For Lukas ❧ A.V.

Text copyright © 1935 by Elizabeth Coatsworth Beston.
Illustrations copyright © 1997 by Anna Vojtech.
The poem used for the text of this book was first published
under the title "Song of the Camels (Twelfth Night)."

Published in the United States by North-South Books Inc., New York.
Published simultaneously in Great Britain, Canada, Australia, and
New Zealand in 1997 by North-South Books, an imprint of
Nord-Süd Verlag AG, Gossau Zürich, Switzerland.

Library of Congress Cataloging-in-Publication Data is available.
A CIP catalogue record for this book is available from The British Library.

The artwork consists of oil paintings on canvas.
Typography by Marc Cheshire

ISBN 1-55858-811-6 (trade binding)
1 3 5 7 9 TB 10 8 6 4 2
ISBN 1-55858-812-4 (library binding)
1 3 5 7 9 LB 10 8 6 4 2
Printed in Belgium

Song of the Camels

A CHRISTMAS POEM BY

Elizabeth Coatsworth

ILLUSTRATED BY

Anna Vojtech

North-South Books

NEW YORK · LONDON

Not born to the forest are we,

Not born to the plain,

To the grass and the shadowing tree

And the splashing of rain.

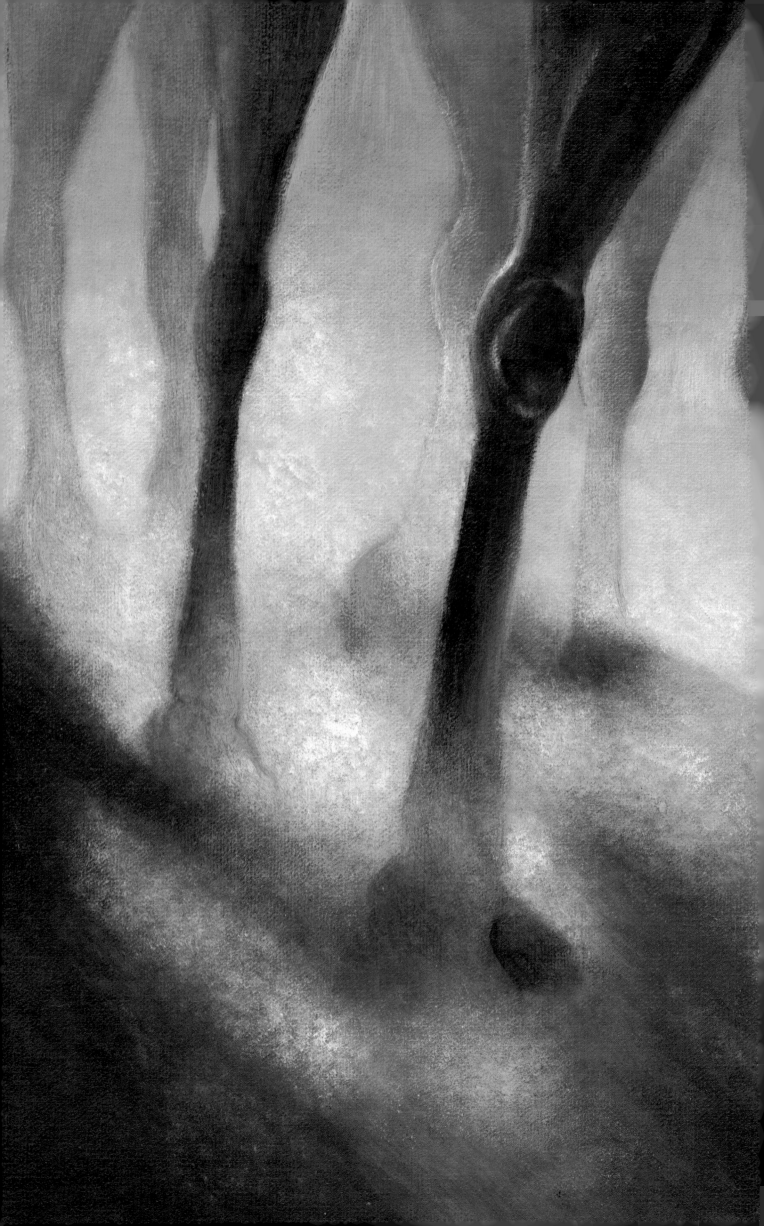

Only the sand we know
And the cloudless sky,

The mirage and the deep-sunk well

And the stars on high.

To the sound of our bells we came
With huge soft stride,

Kings riding upon our backs,
Slaves at our side.

Out of the east drawn on

By a dream and a star,

Seeking the hills and the groves

Where the fixed towns are.

Our goal was no palace gate,
No temple of old,

But a child on his mother's lap

In the cloudy cold.

The olives were windy and white,

Dust swirled through the town,

As all in their royal robes

Our masters knelt down.

Then back to the desert we paced

In our phantom state,

And faded again in the sands

That are secret as fate—

Portents of glory and danger

Our dark shadows lay

At the feet of the babe in the manger

And then drifted away.